PAUL &

ARTHUR

AND THE
·LITTLE·
EXPLORER

by Anne Rockwell

PARENTS' MAGAZINE PRESS ∘ NEW YORK

Library of Congress Cataloging in Publication Data
Rockwell, Anne F.
    Paul and Arthur and the little explorer.
    SUMMARY: Paul and Arthur explore their island with
a little girl who comes ashore from her yacht.
    [1. Islands—Fiction] I. Title.
PZ7.R5943Pau   [E]   72-463
ISBN 0-8193-0592-8   ISBN 0-8193-0593-6 (lib. bdg.)

For Hannah, Elizabeth & Oliver

One fine sunny morning, after breakfast, Paul and Arthur decide that they should have a flag-raising ceremony. The air is fresh and clear, and they have just finished making a big silk flag for their island.

While they are raising the flag the rope
gets stuck, and Paul shinnies up the flagpole
to fix it. He looks out at the blue water
where the fishes swim and play, and suddenly
he sees something very unusual.

Someone is coming ashore in a dinghy!
Who can it be?

Paul and Arthur are so excited. They come down the cliff onto the sandy beach as fast as they can.

It is a little girl in a pink dress and
orange life jacket, with a green knapsack
on her back. Paul feels shy, so Arthur
asks her, "Who are you, and where do you
come from? I am Arthur the bull and this
is my friend Paul."

"My name is Victoria," she says, removing
her life jacket, "and I come from the
Corlione. It is a big boat called a yacht.
Mommy lives on it and Daddy and the captain,
Mr. Jones, and Dooley, the cook, and Topaz,
my cat. I live there, too. I sleep in an
upper berth, but Topaz likes the lower
berth. When I saw this island I decided
to come and explore it."

Paul and Arthur think it is very nice
to have a guest. Their island is far away
from any other island, and sometimes the
pirates come to visit, but little girls
never do.
So off they go, all three, to explore
the island.

"Do you have unicorns here?" asks Victoria, and Paul says, "No, no unicorns, but we have an iguana. Sometimes he pretends to be a dragon, but he's not, really."
And so they take her down the beach a way to the secret lair where Barcello, the great iguana, lives. He pays no attention to them, but sits and thinks, and watches the little flies go by.

Victoria is thirsty, so they climb the
cliff to the hill where the little spring
bubbles up. Each one takes a drink of the
cool, sparkling water from the tin cup.
"Hello, my good friends," calls Mrs. Seagull
from just above.
"Hello, Mrs. Seagull. This is Victoria,"
they answer. "She's come to explore the
island."
And so they set off again, and they
discover . . .

A sleeping owl	A starfish
A big, green beetle	A prickly pear

A banana tree

A quiet snake

A singing cardinal

And a rusty key.

Then they see Old Roland, the mountain goat, just ahead. He is very busy tending his bees. They approach him on tiptoe so as not to disturb him, and then Old Roland turns and offers them some crackers and honeycomb. How hungry they are!

The honeycomb is delicious. It tastes
just as sweet as the meadow smells. After
they have finished, Paul takes out his
harmonica and plays. Arthur, Old Roland
and Victoria sing,

Over the hills and a great way off,
The wind shall blow my topknot off.

Old Roland returns to his work, and they
go back to the beach. Some pirates
are burying their treasure in the sand and
one calls out, "Hey, little girl, if your name
is Victoria, I think your mother's calling."
"Well," says Victoria, "I have to finish
exploring, you know." And she runs to
catch up with Paul and Arthur just ahead.
The pirates shrug their shoulders and go
back to their digging.

They take their shoes off and wade in the ocean. The waves go in and out over their toes and hooves. Shells and seaweed and polished pebbles wash in around them, and little crabs scurry to and fro.

Suddenly Victoria calls out, "Oh, Paul, Arthur, look!"

What has she found? It looks like a piece of a sea-growing tree.

"One, two, three, four, five, six," says Arthur. "Victoria you've found a six-branched coral. Aren't you lucky though."

"Mommy will love this," says Victoria.
"So I think I'll go home now."
She carefully puts it into her knapsack
and they all start back to the dinghy.

But what is happening in the sky above? Where the hot sun was there are now big gray clouds, and far off they can hear thunder. Paul feels a drop of rain on his face, and then another, and suddenly— with a crack of lightning, the rain falls out of the clouds as fast as it can.

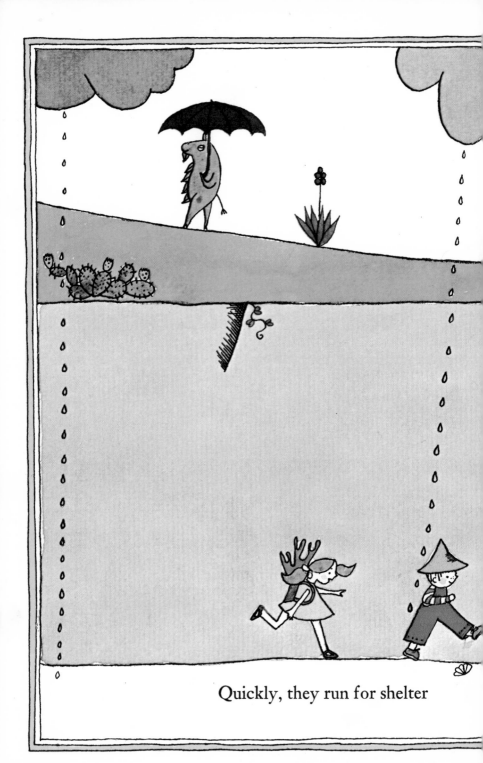

Quickly, they run for shelter

in a nearby cave.

It is dry but dark in the cave. Arthur
takes a few sticks of driftwood and builds
a small fire for them. Their clothes are
wet, and the fire feels warm and cozy.
Paul calls, "Hello!"
And from far off the cave's echo answers,

Hello . . . hello . . . hello . . . hellooooo . . .

They watch the storm on the water. Then
they see a boat on the horizon. It is the
Corlione, slowly gliding through the gray
and misty sea. Someone is calling,
"Victoria, where are you?"
She tries to answer, but no one can hear her.

Victoria is sad. How will she get home now? It is raining too hard and the waves are too big to go out in the little dinghy. Paul and Arthur tell her that she may live with them if she likes, but a tear rolls down her cheek just the same.

And then with joyful surprise, Paul calls,
"Look, everyone! Look, a rainbow!"

As quickly as it began, the storm is over. The sun shines, the air clears, the waves calm. After Arthur has put out the fire, they hurry to the spot where Victoria beached her dinghy.

Here it is. There is rainwater in it, but
they set to and bail it out with some big
clam shells.

"Will you come back and explore with us
again?" they ask her.

"I hope so, because it's fun, and you are
both very nice, and I like you. Maybe my
daddy will come with me next time."

And now the boat is empty and ready for the
journey.

She puts on the life jacket, gets in, takes
the oars in her hands, and Paul and Arthur
push the dinghy into the water. Paul gives
her a cracker he has saved from lunch.
"Good-bye . . . Good-bye," she calls.
They watch until Victoria is past the
rolling surf and safely on her way home.

Then they go back up the cliff

to finish raising the island flag.

Anne Rockwell has both written and illustrated many other beautiful books for young readers, including *Gypsy Girl's Best Shoes*, *When the Drum Sang*, *The Monkey's Whiskers* and *Tuhurahura and the Whale*, all published by Parents' Magazine Press. Also for our list she has illustrated *A Gift for Tolum*, *Mexicali Soup*, *The Glass Valentine*, *The Three Visitors* and *Eric and the Little Canal Boat*. Mrs. Rockwell lives in Old Greenwich, Connecticut, with her husband, artist Harlow Rockwell, and their three children.